I AM READING

Friends Forever

SALLY GRINDLEY

ILLUSTRATED BY

PENNY DANN

KINGFISHER
BOSTON

KINGFISHER
a Houghton Mifflin Company imprint
222 Berkeley Street
Boston, Massachusetts 02116
www.houghtonmifflinbooks.com

First published in 2007
2 4 6 8 10 9 7 5 3 1

These stories first published by Kingfisher as
What Are Friends For? (1998) and *What Will I Do Without You?* (1999)

Text copyright © Sally Grindley 1998, 1999, 2007
Illustrations copyright © Penny Dann 1998, 1999, 2007

LIBRARY OF CONGRESS CATALOGING-IN-PUBLICATION DATA
has been applied for.

ISBN 978-0-7534-5976-8

Printed in China
1TR/1206/WKT/SC(SC)/115MA/C

Contents

What Are Friends For?

Jefferson Bear and Figgy Twosocks
went walking one day in the sunny
green woods.

"J. B.," asked Figgy Twosocks,
"are you my friend?"

"Yes," said Jefferson Bear. "I am your friend, and you are my friend."

"But what is a friend for?" asked Figgy Twosocks.

"Well . . ." said Jefferson Bear.

"A friend is for playing."

"Goody," said Figgy Twosocks. "Let's play play hide-and-seek."

Figgy Twosocks hid in a hollow tree.

Jefferson Bear looked everywhere, but he couldn't find her.

When it was his turn, Jefferson Bear hid
behind a tree stump. Figgy Twosocks
found him right away.
"You're better at this
than me," said
Jefferson Bear.

"I'll help you this time," said Figgy
Twosocks.
She hid under a pile of leaves,
but left the tip of her
tail showing.

The next day, Figgy Twosocks asked,

"J. B., what else is a friend for?"

"Well," said Jefferson Bear, "a friend is

for sharing."

"What do *best* friends share?" asked Figgy Twosocks.

"Well," said Jefferson Bear, "best friends share their favorite things."

Figgy Twosocks darted off through the woods. When she came back, she was tugging on an enormous branch covered with blackberries.

"Would you like some, J. B.?" she asked.

"Blackberries are my favorite.

Yummy, aren't they?"

"De-licious," said

Jefferson Bear.

That afternoon, loud squeals woke up
Jefferson Bear from his sleep.

Yelp! Yelp! Yelp! Yelp! Yelp!

"I'm coming," he
bellowed. "What's
the matter?"

He found Figgy Twosocks lying on
the ground.

"You've got a thorn in your foot.
Stay still, and I'll take it out."

"Will it hurt?" whimpered Figgy.

"I'll be as gentle as I can," said Jefferson
Bear. He closed his teeth around the
thorn and pulled.

As soon as it was out, Figgy Twosocks
jumped up and pranced around.

"Thank you for helping me, J. B.," she said.

"That's what friends are for," said

Jefferson Bear.

The next afternoon, Jefferson Bear was
dozing in the sun. Figgy Twosocks
wanted to play. She crept up behind
him and yelled . . .

"Boo!"

Jefferson Bear almost jumped out of his fur. Figgy Twosocks ran around and around squealing, "Made you jump! Made you jump!"

Jefferson Bear didn't think it was funny.

"Go away, Figgy Twosocks," he said.

"You have made me angry."

"But I want to play," said Figgy Twosocks.

"And I want to sleep," said Jefferson Bear.

"A big brown bear needs his sleep.

Go and play somewhere else."

"You're not my friend anymore,"
said Figgy Twosocks sadly, and she
trudged off.

When Jefferson Bear woke
up the next morning,
he felt sorry that he had
upset his friend.
"I'll play with her today,"
he said to himself.
But Figgy Twosocks stayed away.
Jefferson Bear began to worry. He went
to her den and called, "Figgy Twosocks,
are you all right?"

There was no reply.

Jefferson Bear's worry grew.

He walked to the edge of the river

and called again, "Where are you,

Figgy Twosocks?"

But there was no reply.

Jefferson Bear's worry grew bigger.

He walked through the woods calling,

"Come out, Figgy Twosocks. It's me,

Jefferson Bear."

But there was still no reply.

At last he came to a hollow
tree where he saw the tip
of a tail sticking out.
"Figgy Twosocks, is that you?"
he called. "It's J.B."
He listened and thought
that he heard a sniff.

The sniff grew louder and louder—until it turned into a

GREAT BIG SOB.

"Figgy Twosocks, please come out," said Jefferson Bear. "I miss you."

"I'm sorry, J.B.," said Figgy Twosocks. "I didn't mean to make you angry."

"And I'm sorry I was so grumpy," said Jefferson Bear. "Let's go and play."

"J.B.," said Figgy Twosocks with a sniff, "does that mean you're still my friend?"

"Of course I'm still your friend," said Jefferson Bear. "A friend is forever."

What Will I Do Without You?

Winter was on its way. Jefferson Bear was fat, and his fur was softer than ever.

"Should we go for our walk?" asked Figgy Twosocks.

"No time to walk, Figgy," said Jefferson Bear. "I'm getting ready to hibernate."

"What's hibernate?" asked Figgy.

"Hibernate is what big brown bears do in the winter," said Jefferson Bear. "It's when I go to sleep and don't wake up until the spring."

"But what will I do without you?" asked Figgy.

"I'll be back before you know it," said Jefferson Bear.

The air turned frosty.

"Time for bed," yawned Jefferson Bear.

"Don't go yet," said Figgy Twosocks.

But Jefferson Bear hugged her tight

and disappeared inside his cave.

"I'll miss you, J.B.," called Figgy.

The next morning, it was snowing.

Figgy had never seen snow before.

She ran to tell Jefferson Bear.

"J. B., are you asleep yet?" she called.

A rumbly snore echoed from deep inside his cave.

Figgy kicked at the snow.

ZZZ ZZZ ZZZ!

"What good is snow when your best friend isn't there to share it?"

BIFF! BIFF! BIFF!

Figgy's brothers were
having a snowball fight.

"Can I play?" Figgy Twosocks asked.

"If you want," said Big Smudge.

"Take this," said Floppylugs.

BIFF!

"Stop it!" Figgy squealed. "That hurts."
"You wanted to play," they said
and ran off laughing.
"You wouldn't do that if
J. B. was here," she cried.

Then Figgy Twosocks had an idea . . .
All day long she
pushed and patted
the snow.

All day long she rolled and scooped and
shaped it.

At last, she found three black stones
and a little twig.
She stood back.

"Every time I look at my Big White
Snow Bear, I will think of J. B.," she said.
But Figgy Twosocks still felt very lonely.
She sobbed a great big sob.

Then she began to feel angry.

If J. B. was her friend, how could

he leave her for so long?

PIFF!—she threw a snowball

at the Snow Bear.

PIFF!—and another.

And another—PIFF!

"Hey, don't do that. You'll
spoil it," called a voice.
It was Hoptail, the squirrel.
"J. B.'s not my friend
anymore," said Figgy
Twosocks.

"Why not?" asked Hoptail.
"He's not here when I need him."
"But he needs his sleep," said Hoptail.
"And I need some help. I must find the
nuts that I buried in the fall."

Hoptail pointed to places where she thought her food was hidden.

Figgy Twosocks dug through the snow and earth to find the nuts.

Day after day, more snow fell.

Figgy Twosocks and Hoptail ran through the woods, making patterns with their paw prints.

They broke off
icicles and
watched them
melt in
their paws.

And together they
rebuilt the Big
White Snow Bear.

At the end of each day, Figgy Twosocks went to see the Big White Snow Bear. "I hope J. B. won't mind me having another friend," she said.

Little by little, the days grew warmer.

"The Snow Bear is melting!"

cried Figgy.

"What's happening?"

"Spring is coming,"

said Hoptail.

Suddenly, Big Smudge and Floppylugs

appeared. They clambered onto the Snow

Bear and pushed—

HEAVE . . .

WHOOSH!

The head of the
Snow Bear rolled
down the hill.

"OUCH—that hurt,"
growled a great big voice.

Big Smudge and Floppylugs

ran away.

There was Jefferson Bear, rubbing his nose.

"That's a fine welcome back," he said.

"J. B.!" squealed Figgy.
"Oh, I've missed
you so much.

I built a Snow Bear to
remind me of you, and
I hope you don't
mind, but I've—"
"Yes?" said Jefferson Bear.
"I've made a new friend—this is Hoptail."

Jefferson Bear laughed. "Slow down, Figgy. Let's all go for a walk, and you can tell me everything you did without me."

About the author and illustrator

Sally Grindley is an award-winning author with many books to her name. She has written *Captain Pepper's Pets* and *The Perfect Monster* in the *I Am Reading* series.

Penny Dann has illustrated many books for children. She lives by the sea in a house with a pretty garden. When she's not drawing pictures, she likes to travel around the world.

Strategies for Independent Readers

Predict
Think about the cover, illustrations, and the title of the book. What do you think this book will be about? While you are reading think about what may happen next and why.

Monitor
As you read ask yourself if what you're reading makes sense. If it doesn't, reread, look at the illustrations, or read ahead.

Question
Ask yourself questions about important ideas in the story such as what the characters might do or what you might learn.

Phonics
If there is a word that you do not know, look carefully at the letters, sounds, and word parts that you do know. Blend the sounds to read the word. Ask yourself if this is a word you know. Does it make sense in the sentence?

Summarize
Think about the characters, the setting where the story takes place, and the problem the characters faced in the story. Tell the important ideas in the beginning, middle, and end of the story.

Evaluate
Ask yourself questions like: Did you like the story? Why or why not? How did the author make the story come alive? How did the author make the story fun to read? How well did you understand the story? Maybe you can understand it better if you read it again!